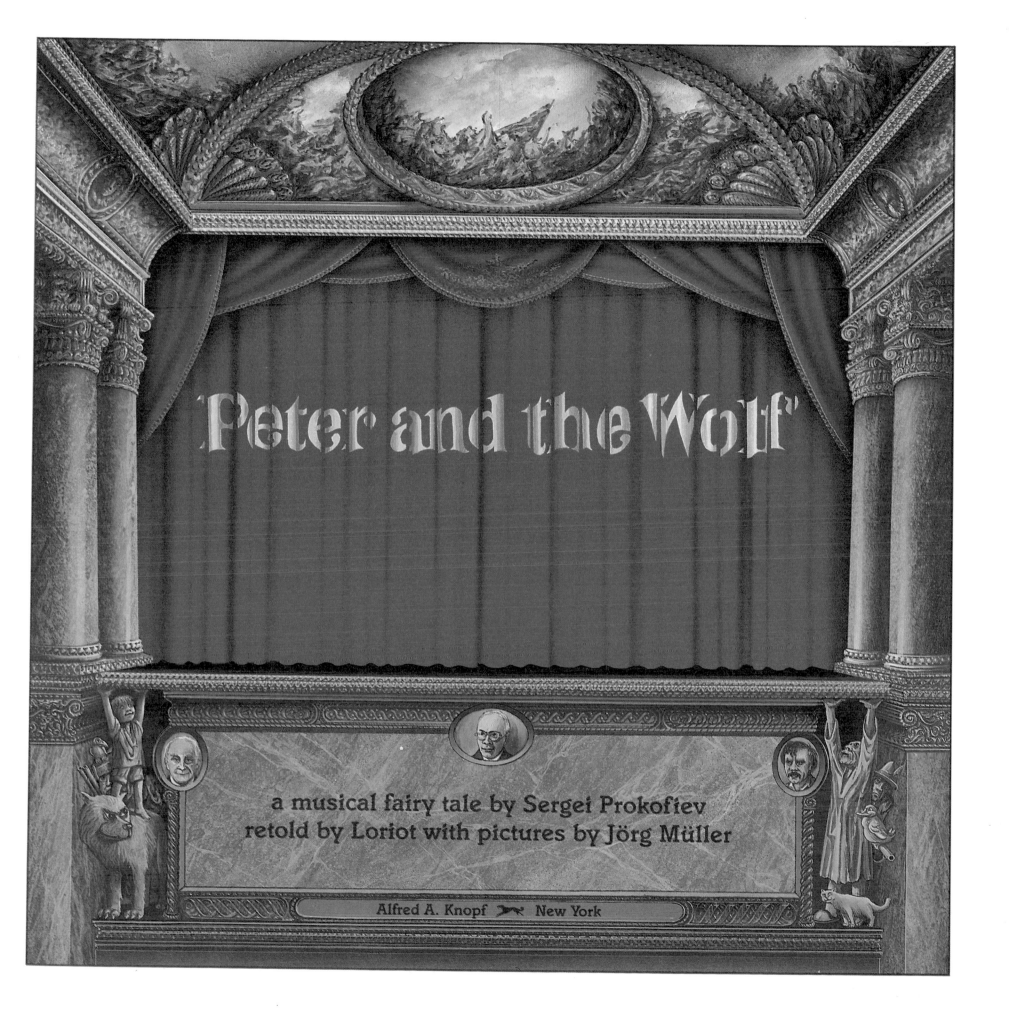

Peter and the Wolf

a musical fairy tale by Sergei Prokofiev
retold by Loriot with pictures by Jörg Müller

Alfred A. Knopf 🐾 New York

THIS IS A BORZOI BOOK
PUBLISHED BY ALFRED A. KNOPF, INC.

Translation copyright © 1986 by Alfred A. Knopf,
Inc. Illustrations copyright © 1985 by Verlag
Sauerländer. All rights reserved under
International and Pan-American Copyright
Conventions. Published in the United States by
Alfred A. Knopf, Inc., New York, and
simultaneously in Canada by Random House of
Canada Limited, Toronto. Distributed by Random
House, Inc., New York. Originally published in
German as *Peter und der Wolf.* German text first
published in Switzerland by Diogenes Verlag AG,
Zurich, in 1983. Copyright © 1983 by Diogenes
Verlag AG, Zurich. Illustrations originally
published simultaneously in Switzerland and
Germany by Verlag Sauerländer in 1985.
Copyright © 1985 by Verlag Sauerländer, Aarau,
Switzerland, and Frankfurt am Main, Germany.
Manufactured in West Germany
10 9 8 7 6 5 4

Library of Congress Cataloging-in-Publication Data
Prokofiev, Sergei, 1891–1953. Peter and the wolf.
Translation of: Petia i volk. Summary: A retelling
of the orchestral fairy tale in which Peter ignores
his grandfather's warnings and proceeds to
capture a wolf. [1. Fairy tales] I. Müller, Jörg, ill.
II. Title. PZ8.P947Pe 1986b [Fic] 86-7462
ISBN 0-394-88417-5 (book);
ISBN 0-679-86156-4 (book and cassette pkg.)

Peter and the Wolf—a musical fairy tale in which all the characters are represented by different instruments of the orchestra:

the bird by the flute,

the duck by the oboe,

the cat by the clarinet,

the grandfather by the bassoon,

the wolf by three French horns,

Peter by all the strings of the orchestra,

and the gunshots by the kettle drums and the big bass drum.

Our story begins one morning while the fat duck and the grandfather were still sleeping. Peter quietly opened the garden gate and went out into the meadow.

In a tall tree in front of the garden wall sat a little bird who was Peter's friend. He called out:

Do you hear how quiet it is?

Meanwhile, the fat duck had awakened and saw that the garden gate was open. "Ah," she thought, "the day has begun well. Now I can have my bath in the pond in the meadow." And off she waddled, right past the little bird.

They argued and argued, the duck paddling in the water, the bird skipping about on the shore.

Suddenly Peter, who was watching nearby, saw the cat sneaking through the grass.

"How I love birds," thought the cat, "especially for breakfast with white bread and milk."

"Look out!" cried Peter.

As quick as lightning the bird flew up into the tree—

while the duck quacked and stuck her tongue out at the cat...from the middle of the pond. "You will regret that," thought the cat, licking her lips.

Now the grandfather woke up and stomped out the garden gate to look for Peter.

Shame on you, Peter.

"I have forbidden you to go into the meadow alone. What if the wolf should come out of the forest? What would you do then?"

"But I'm not afraid of the wolf," said Peter.

Sternly the grandfather took Peter's hand, went back into the garden, and locked the gate.

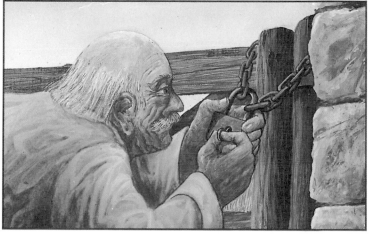

"If the wolf comes, I will protect Peter," the grandfather thought as he lay back in bed and fell asleep.

And then it happened. Out of the forest came the big gray wolf!

The cat hissed and raced up the tree… as high as she could go.

But the foolish duck sprang out of the water and stuck her tongue out at the wolf! Then she tried to run away.

The wolf snarled, "You dare to tease *me*!" And he came nearer…and nearer…

and he pounced on the duck…

and swallowed her whole!

The cat and the bird watched from the tree. "Now the wolf has his eye on you," said the bird to the cat. "And I have my eye on you," answered the cat.

The wolf planted himself under the tree.

Come, let's play...

said the wolf in a friendly voice as he stared up at the cat with his big red eyes.

Peter was watching through the locked garden gate. "I'm not afraid of the wolf," he whispered, and he ran off toward the house. In no time at all he returned with a rope and climbed up the garden gate and onto the stone wall. Then he grabbed hold of a branch and swung up into the tree.

"Don't just sit there," he called softly to the little bird. "Tickle the wolf's nose for me. But don't let him catch hold of you!" The little bird said:

Well, I'd rather tease the wolf than be eaten by the cat.

So he flew down and perched on the wolf's nose.

A bird on the nose is better than a cat in a tree…

thought the wolf.

So he snapped at the bird. But the bird fluttered back and forth above the wolf just out of reach. The wolf snapped and snapped, again and again, but he still could not catch him.

Meanwhile, Peter had tied a noose on one end of the rope. And when the wolf came near, Peter slipped the noose over the wolf's tail.

When the tail was nicely in place, Peter pulled the line toward him.

"I'll just tug on this line," snarled the wolf, "and pull the child down. Then I will eat him." And the wolf pulled and pulled.

But Peter had tied the line solidly to the tree. The wolf growled.

He tugged and pulled savagely on the rope until he lay on the ground exhausted.

"Please let me go home," pleaded the wolf. "And I will never ever come here again."

Scarcely had he said that when the hunters crept out of the forest! They were afraid of the wolf and had spent the entire morning eating and drinking.

When they saw the wolf…

they were terrified and shot into the air.

"Stop that shooting!" cried Peter. "We have caught the wolf and we are taking him back to the forest." The hunters were ashamed of themselves.

Come with me!

chirped the bird. And then everyone started for the forest with the wolf.

First came Peter.

Behind him marched the hunters with fearful faces...

and the big, tired wolf!

And last came the grandfather with the cat.

The grandfather was thinking, "If the wolf hadn't eaten the duck, we could have had her for dinner." And the cat was thinking, "Tomorrow I'm going to catch that bird."

The little bird flew over them and chirped:

Today I tickled the wolf, tomorrow I will tickle the cat!

The duck sat comfortably in the wolf's belly.

At last I can travel peacefully...

she thought, and she stuck her tongue out at the wolf.